THE
SPOTTED PONY

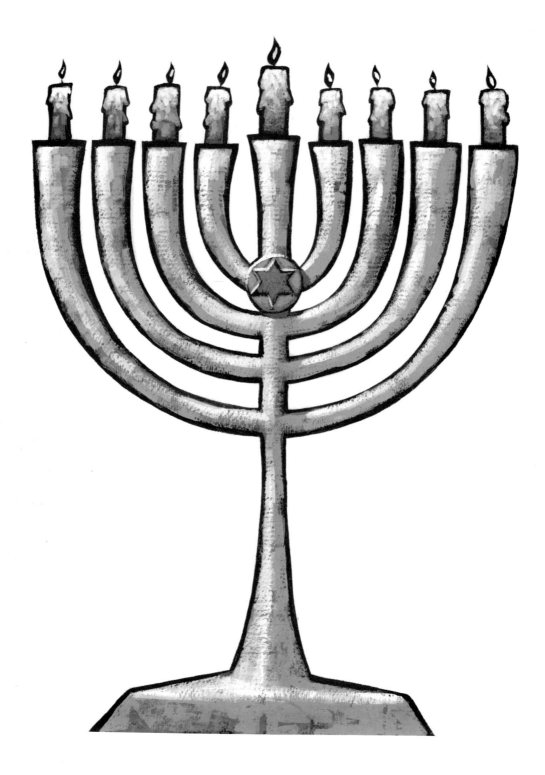

THE SPOTTED PONY

A Collection of Hanukkah Stories

retold by Eric A. Kimmel

illustrated by Leonard Everett Fisher

Holiday House/New York

For Margery

Library of Congress Cataloging-in-Publication Data
Kimmel, Eric A.
The spotted pony : a collection of Hanukkah stories / by Eric A. Kimmel ;
illustrated by Leonard Everett Fisher.
p. cm.
Summary: Eight stories, with a "shammes" story for each, to be
read on the eight nights of Hanukkah.
ISBN 0-8234-0936-8
[1. Jews—Fiction.] I. Fisher, Leonard Everett, ill. II. Title.
PZ7.K5648Sp   1992   91-24214   CIP   AC
[Fic]—dc20

CONTENTS

Once Upon a Time...

My grandmother was a great storyteller. That was why my family had a unique way of celebrating Hanukkah. After lighting the candles, Nana would tell a story. She told a different one on each of the eight nights of Hanukkah. Just as a *shammes* or "servant" candle is used to light others, so she would begin with a little *shammes* story as an introduction.

What stories they were! King Solomon and his magic ring, Benayahu ben Yehoyada, the bravest of the brave, and Ashmodai, king of the demons. We heard about Hershel of Ostropol, that clever trickster, and the poor people of Chelm, who were always putting two and two together to make five. There were tales of birds and animals, magicians and princes, miracle-working saints and ghostly spirits.

After I started school, I would pore through all the books in the library, looking for stories I could tell. I began preparing months in advance. By the time Hanukkah arrived, my head would be stuffed with stories. I would try to match Nana tale for tale. Yet no matter how many I knew, she always knew one more. Once I asked her to tell me her secret. Where did she learn so many stories? She couldn't read English. She didn't go to the library. She answered, "The stories you know, you learned from books. I learned my stories through my eyes and ears."

Here then are eight stories, with a *shammes* for each, that I've learned through my eyes and ears, as Nana told them to me.

In the Beginning

A long time ago, whenever the great Rabbi Israel ben Eliezer, the Master of the Good Name, faced an unsolvable problem, he would go to a certain place in the forest. There he would light a fire and say special prayers. And he would receive the answer he sought.

Years later, his successor, Rabbi Dov Baer of Mezritch, would also go to that same place in the forest. He no longer knew how to light the fire, but he would say the prayers. And he too would receive the answer.

By the time of Rabbi Israel of Rizhin, the location of the place in the forest was forgotten. So was the ceremony for lighting the fire. But Rabbi Israel would say the prayers. And the answer would come.

We can no longer find the place in the forest. We do not remember how to light the fire. We have forgotten the prayers. But we can still tell the story.

And the answer will come.

First Night

SHAMMES

*A*braham Ibn Ezra once visited the sultan of Egypt. Exquisite murals decorated the walls of the sultan's palace. One wall, however, was blank. The sultan explained: "Karaguz, the master artist, painted these murals two hundred years ago. He died before he could finish the last one. Since then, this wall has remained blank. No artist has attempted to paint it, for none can equal Karaguz's skill."

"I can paint this wall for you," said Ibn Ezra. "When complete, it will surpass the others. Furthermore, I will do it in one day."

"What magic will you use to work this miracle?" the sultan asked, convinced that Ibn Ezra was joking.

Ibn Ezra replied: "No magic at all. I need only powdered silver, antimony, a pile of clean rags, and most important, a curtain to hide my work from prying eyes."

The sultan's servants brought Ibn Ezra all he required. Ibn Ezra mixed the silver and antimony into a paste. He spread the paste on the empty wall. After it dried, he polished it with the rags. Then he sent for the sultan.

"Is the mural finished?" the sultan asked.

"It is," Ibn Ezra replied.

"And does it surpass the work of Karaguz?"

"Judge for yourself."

Ibn Ezra swept the curtain aside. A bright mirror gleamed on the surface of the once-empty wall, reflecting the paintings on the other walls in such a way that they seemed alive—a quality that all the skill of Karaguz had never been known to equal.

11

Ibn Ezra and
the Archbishop

Rabbi Abraham Ibn Ezra lived in the Middle Ages. At a time when few people journeyed more than a few miles from their birthplace, Ibn Ezra traveled the whole world, from Baghdad to Rome. He spoke Latin, Greek, and Arabic as well as he spoke Hebrew, and knew many other languages besides.

Once, on a journey from Spain to Egypt, his ship was captured by pirates. Ibn Ezra was taken to the French port of Nice and sold as a slave. He passed from one master to another until he came to England. A steward of the archbishop of Canterbury purchased him and set him to work in the kitchen of the archbishop's palace. Taking note of Ibn Ezra's skill with the carving knife, the cook assigned him to carve the roast at the archbishop's table.

One evening at dinner the archbishop and several other high church-men began discussing the books of the Bible. They spoke in Latin, the language of the Church.

"Why is it," the archbishop began, "that of Noah the Scripture states, 'he was a righteous man in his generation,' whereas of Abraham it merely says, 'he was a righteous man'?"

None of the other bishops had an answer. Ibn Ezra, carving the roast, spoke up.

"With your permission, my lord Archbishop, I believe I can explain that."

The churchmen looked at him in surprise, for they were unused to servants speaking Latin and taking part in their discussions.

"You may speak," the archbishop said.

Ibn Ezra bowed. "Noah appears righteous only in comparison to the people of his generation, who were exceptionally wicked. He would not have been considered righteous had he lived at another time. Abraham, on the other hand, would have been righteous in any age."

The archbishop and his fellow churchmen nodded in agreement, for Ibn Ezra's answer explained both verses perfectly. "How did you come to possess such learning?" the archbishop asked.

"I am a rabbi, a teacher and scholar of the Jewish faith," Ibn Ezra replied. "Captured by pirates, I was sold as a slave. I pray that one day the Lord will redeem me from captivity."

"Your prayers are answered," the archbishop said. "If you agree to become a Christian, I will free you at once. Our Church welcomes men of learning. There is no limit to how high you might rise. I think it not unlikely that you may someday find yourself seated at this table as one of my bishops."

Ibn Ezra thanked the archbishop, but declined his offer. "I will be true to the faith of my ancestors," he said.

"You are an honest person. I respect that. I will not free you, but I will make the chains of your bondage so light, you will not notice them." The archbishop ordered that Ibn Ezra would no longer work in the kitchen. He would remain at his side as his secretary and the keeper of his library.

Thus began a close friendship between two men of learning that grew and blossomed as the years went by.

King John ruled England in those days. He called himself a Christian, but in truth he had no use for the Church's teachings. Time and again the good archbishop of Canterbury condemned his greed and violence. King John decided to rid himself of this troublesome archbishop and appoint one of his henchmen in his place. He summoned the archbishop to London, where he upbraided him before the entire court as a man of little learning who was unfit to hold such a high position.

"Why, you cannot answer the simplest questions! Tell me, for example, in which direction does God face? What is a king worth? And what does he think?"

"These are not simple questions, Your Majesty," the archbishop replied. "I must have time to think about them."

"You could not find the answers if you took a hundred years!" King John laughed, and his court of flatterers laughed with him. He said to the archbishop, "If, in thirty days, you cannot answer correctly, I will throw you in prison."

The archbishop returned to Canterbury, deeply distressed. King John's questions were not simple at all. They were carefully phrased so as to be impossible to answer. If the archbishop were to say that God faced west, King John could answer, "No, He faces east." What was a king worth? If the archbishop said a thousand crowns, King John could answer, "No, a thousand and one," or "Nine hundred and ninety-nine." As to what a king thought, who could answer that? John was the only king in England, and he was so sly that no one could ever tell what he was thinking. The archbishop saw no way to avoid his fate. In thirty days' time he would be thrown in a dungeon. One of John's flatterers would become archbishop of Canterbury. Who would protect the good people of England then?

Ibn Ezra noticed the archbishop's despair. He asked what was troubling him. The archbishop told him the three impossible riddles, adding, "I daresay not one person in all of England knows the answers."

"That is not true, my lord," Ibn Ezra replied. "There is one, and he is nearer at hand than you think."

"Who is he?"

"Myself!" said Ibn Ezra. "Lend me your robes and your traveling cloak, and I will bring King John the answers he seeks."

Thirty days later Ibn Ezra set out for London dressed as the archbishop of Canterbury. He pulled the traveling cloak's hood over his head to hide his face. Thus attired, he came before King John.

"I trust you have the answers to my questions, my lord Archbishop. If not, so much the worse for you," King John said.

"I will do my best," Ibn Ezra replied, disguising his voice so that he sounded like the archbishop.

"In what direction does God turn his face?"

Ibn Ezra plucked a torch from an iron sconce. "In what direction does this torch shine its light?"

"In all directions," the king said.

"So too with God. His face is turned to all Creation."

King John muttered and fumed, but he could not challenge that answer. He proceeded to the second question: "What am I worth?"

Ibn Ezra did not hesitate to reply. "Exactly three pennies."

"How can I, a king, be worth so little?"

Ibn Ezra took a holy medal from his purse. "Your Majesty, is this the image of the God you worship?"

King John admitted it was so.

"I bought this image for four pence at Canterbury Cathedral. If that is God's value, I would estimate yours to be a penny less."

King John could not say he was worth more than God, and he could not bring himself to say he was worth less than three pence, so he had to accept the answer. His mouth twisted into a tight grin, giving him the look of a cat about to pounce.

"Two riddles well answered. One more, my lord Archbishop, and you may return in peace to Canterbury. Tell me, if you can, what do I think?"

Ibn Ezra threw back the hood. "You think I am the archbishop of Canterbury, but I am only Abraham Ibn Ezra, his friend and servant."

"Get you hence!" King John swept from the room with his henchmen at his heels.

The bells of Canterbury Cathedral rang out to welcome Abraham Ibn Ezra. "All England is in your debt, myself most of all," the archbishop told him. He asked Ibn Ezra's forgiveness.

"How so, my lord?" Ibn Ezra asked.

"I should have freed you at once. It was wrong to keep you a slave. From this moment you are a free man."

Ibn Ezra kissed the archbishop's hand. "Slave or free, I will happily remain in your service."

"No, my friend Abraham," the archbishop said. "King John is a cunning man who never forgives those who have bested him. I fear that England has become a dangerous place for you. You must leave at once. I have hired a ship to take you wherever you wish to go. It is waiting."

And so Abraham Ibn Ezra left England with the blessings of the archbishop of Canterbury and the gratitude of the good people of that country. However, his adventures were not ended. The tale of how his ship sank off the coast of Spain and how Ibn Ezra entered the service of the king of Granada can be read in the book *The Journeys of Abraham*. But that is another story.

Second Night

SHAMMES

*T*wo thieves broke into a barn one night. The first rode away on the farmer's donkey. The second climbed into the donkey's stall and stood with the animal's bridle pulled over his head.

"Who are you? Where is my donkey?" the farmer cried when he entered the barn the next morning.

The thief replied: "Master, don't you recognize me? I am your donkey. Years ago I had a fight with a witch. I called her bad names. She put a curse on me. I had to spend a year in a donkey's body for each bad word I spoke. The years are up today; the curse is lifted. I am free."

"Who would have thought such miracles possible?" the simple farmer exclaimed. "Go in peace, my donkey. Take your freedom, now that you are a human being again." The farmer gave the thief some money to start his new life, and some advice as well. "Think before you speak. There is no excuse for using bad language. Go now, and may you profit from your misfortune."

The thief thanked the farmer. Then he rushed off to join his companion at the market, where they sold the donkey for a good price.

Late that afternoon the farmer too went to market. There he encountered his old donkey standing with a FOR SALE sign around its neck.

The farmer boxed the poor donkey's ears. "Idiot! Didn't I warn you to watch your mouth? Now you're back where you started."

The Kabil's Donkey

The town of Hanin lies high in the mountains of Yemen. Jews have lived there since the time of King Solomon.

It once happened that the governor of the district appointed a kabil, a minor official, to take charge of Hanin's affairs. This man's wickedness was exceeded only by his stupidity. He could not bear to see Jews living in peace with their Muslim neighbors, so he set about causing trouble.

He summoned the leaders of the Jewish community and told them he had discovered a forgotten law requiring all Jewish orphans to be raised as Muslims. He notified the Jews of Hanin that he intended to begin enforcing it.

Only Mar Saadiyah, the teacher at the orphanage, did not express concern. "Leave the kabil to me," he told the children. "When a person acts like a jackass, he usually thinks like one."

Some days later the kabil rode his donkey up to the orphanage. He found Mar Saadiyah and the orphans sitting beneath the fig tree.

"I've come for the orphans," the kabil announced.

Mar Saadiyah looked around. "There are no orphans here."

The kabil scowled. "The children sitting under this tree are orphans."

"They are not orphans," Mar Saadiyah said. "They are donkeys."

"What?"

"Donkeys," Mar Saadiyah repeated. "All the orphans ran away when they heard they were going to be forced to change their religion. I had to keep busy, so I started teaching the donkeys in the neighboring field. After a few days, something astonishing happened. The donkeys began to change shape. They didn't look like donkeys anymore. They looked like children. The more they studied, the more like children they became. Unfortunately, the change isn't permanent. If they ever stop studying, they will become donkeys again."

The kabil could not believe his ears. "Can a donkey become a human being? Can it happen to this old jackass of mine?"

Mar Saadiyah examined the kabil's donkey. "I'm not sure. That's an old, stubborn beast. I'm willing to try. Leave your donkey here. I'll see what I can do."

The kabil was delighted. "I'll come by next month to check his progress."

"I trust you'll be pleased," Mar Saadiyah said.

After the kabil left, Mar Saadiyah and the orphans drove the old donkey to the next town. They sold him to a candy merchant for two sacks of halvah and one sack of pistachio nuts. Then they had a grand feast, courtesy of the kabil.

The kabil came by a month later. He looked over the orphans. "Which one of these donkeys is mine?" he asked Mar Saadiyah.

"He's not here."

"Where is he? What have you done with him?"

"Nothing. Your donkey did it himself. You should be proud of him. Within a week he learned everything I had to teach. I sent him on to the college at Tarim. He graduated last week. The governor came to see this amazing donkey. He was so impressed he appointed him judge in Demar. I received a letter from him the other day. He sent his regards. He'd like to see you again. He asked you to drop by the courthouse the next time you're in Demar."

The kabil's head spun. Could such things happen? Could a donkey go to college and be appointed a judge? He set out for Demar to see for himself. When he arrived, he went straight to the courthouse.

Now it so happened that the judge in Demar had long, hairy ears. Seen in the right light, he looked a bit like a donkey.

The kabil strode into the courthouse and saw what he thought was his old donkey seated on the judge's bench. "Congratulations, you old jackass!" he called from the back of the courtroom. "I see you've come up in the world."

The judge raised his head. "Whom do you think you're talking to?"

"Come now, don't play the fool," the kabil chuckled. "You know perfectly well who I am. You carried me on your back for fifteen years . . ."

"What!"

". . . and your mother used to sleep in my stable!"

"Insult my mother? You'll pay for this!" The judge turned to the bailiffs of the court. "Take this impudent rascal outside. Cut off his head!"

The bailiffs drew their swords. The kabil fled from the courtroom with the bailiffs at his heels. Fortunately, he was faster than they were. Even so, he barely escaped with his life.

The kabil ran all the way back to Hanin. He didn't stop until he reached the orphanage. He found Mar Saadiyah sitting under the fig tree, teaching his "donkeys" their lessons.

"Stop what you are doing!" the kabil cried.

"What is wrong?" Mar Saadiyah asked.

"You mustn't teach these donkeys anymore. I warn you, Mar Saadiyah, they are not the gentle beasts they pretend to be. They are ruthless and cunning. I have just escaped from Demar. Would you believe it? My own donkey lured me there so he could cut off my head!"

"No!"

"It's true. Once a jackass gets power, there is no controlling him. I tell you, Mar Saadiyah, unless we stop them now, these donkeys will take over the world. There will be no humans left. Only jackasses."

"I see," Mar Saadiyah said. "But what can I do? I am a teacher. I cannot sit idle. Who will I teach if I can't teach the donkeys?"

"Call back the orphans," the kabil said. "I learned my lesson. I won't meddle again."

The kabil was true to his word. From that day on the Jews and Muslims of Hanin lived together in peace, and Mar Saadiyah and the children sat beneath the fig tree studying their lessons undisturbed.

Third Night

SHAMMES

*I*n the days when the Romans ruled the land of Israel, the Emperor Hadrian issued a decree outlawing the Torah. Henceforth anyone caught studying God's word or teaching it to others would suffer torture and death. The great Rabbi Akiba and his students fled to the desert to continue studying the Torah at the risk of their lives. The Romans pursued them relentlessly. Rabbi Akiba's students lost hope.

"Rabbi," they said, "how long can we endure running from place to place, hiding in caves, never knowing if each day will be our last? Where is the God of Israel? What use is His Torah? Why do we cling to an empty reed? Let us be like the other nations. Let us bow to the gods of Rome and live."

Rabbi Akiba replied with a story. "A school of fish once fled across a lake. Bigger fish pursued them from below, while boats of fishermen cast their nets at them from above. The fish found shelter in a quiet cove. A hungry fox came by. He noticed the fish swimming just beyond reach. In a voice filled with compassion, he spoke to them:

"Poor fish! Why live in this lake with danger everywhere? Take my advice. Leave the lake. Come up on dry land. You will be safe here."

The fish replied to the fox: "Your words are true. Life is difficult for us in the lake. But living on dry land is impossible."

Then Rabbi Akiba said, "The Torah is the lake, the fox is the emperor of Rome, and the people of Israel are the little fish. Life may be difficult for us as long as we cling to the Torah. But without it, how could we live at all?"

Leviathan and the Fox

In the beginning of things, when the Lord created the heavens and the earth, He created the great fish, Leviathan, to rule the sea and the wild ox, Behemoth, to rule the land. The Lord gave Leviathan and Behemoth exactly the same number of subjects so that there might be peace between them. Yet within a few days, Leviathan started complaining.

"It isn't fair, Lord! Behemoth is a greater king than I. You promised we would be equal."

"You are equal," the Lord said. "You have exactly the same number of subjects."

"Behemoth's subjects are better than mine. He rules over quick, bright animals. Over whom do I rule? Cold, slimy fish."

"Fish are beautiful in their own way," the Lord replied.

"They are not as clever as animals," Leviathan insisted.

In order to avoid a quarrel between sea and land, the Lord set aside a day when each species of animal would send one of its kind down to the seashore. The dark angel would throw the animals into the water where they would become fish. Thus Leviathan would have exactly the same kind of subjects as Behemoth.

The animals assembled at the seashore on the appointed day. One by one the dark angel cast them into the water where they became fish.

He threw in a cat; it became a catfish.

He threw in a horse; it became a sea horse.

He threw in a lion; it became a sea lion.

So it went throughout the day.

The fox stood at the end of the line. The hot sand prickled his toes. The sun warmed his back. He looked up at the bright blue sky and thought, *Do I really want to leave this beautiful world to become a fish?* The more he considered the idea, the less he liked it. Meanwhile the line grew shorter. Soon the fox's turn would come to stand before the dark angel. *I had better think of something fast,* the fox told himself. After all, he wasn't a fox for nothing.

The fox's turn arrived. The dark angel stooped to pick him up and throw him into the sea, when the fox burst into tears.

"Woe is me! My brother, my poor, poor brother! Alas, I will never see him again!"

"Don't make a scene," the angel chided him. "It is not as if you were dying. You will become a fish and have the whole ocean to swim in. What is wrong with that?"

The fox stared at the angel in terror. "A fish? Surely you do not mean to cast me in too? Not after you just threw in my brother!"

The dark angel had thrown so many animals into the ocean that day he could not remember if one had been a fox or not. "You are mistaken," the angel said. "I did not throw any foxes in."

"But you did. You threw in my poor brother. There he is, waving good-bye below the waves. Good-bye, dear brother, good-bye!" The fox leaned out so that the water's surface mirrored his reflection. The angel looked down and, sure enough, there was a fox staring up at him from the ocean's depths.

"Great Metatron's wings! I nearly threw you in too. You had best say good-bye to your brother and be off. It is dangerous to linger here."

"You are right," the fox said. He scampered off into the hills.

That evening King Leviathan called the roll of his new subjects.

"Sea horse?"

"Here."

"Dogfish?"

"Here."

"Catfish."

"Here."

"Foxfish."

No answer.

"Foxfish?" Leviathan called again. "Where is the fox? There is supposed to be a fox here."

All the fish laughed. They told the king how the fox fooled the dark angel. Leviathan lashed his tail back and forth, but in time his anger cooled. He thought, *If that fox could fool the dark angel, he must be a clever animal indeed. Every creature's cleverness lies in his heart. If I could catch that fox and eat his heart, I would be as clever as he.*

Leviathan began forming a plan.

One bright summer day, as the fox ran along the seashore, he heard a voice booming out over the waves.

"FOX! FOX!"

He looked and saw an enormous whale swimming back and forth along the breakers. The fox jumped up to attract his attention.

"Over here! I'm the fox! What do you want?"

The whale swam close to shore and spouted a cloud of vapor.

"OH, WISE AND CLEVER FOX, MY MASTER, KING LEVIATHAN, SENDS ME TO BRING YOU A MESSAGE. HE HEARD HOW YOU FOOLED THE DARK ANGEL. HE INVITES YOU TO A BANQUET IN YOUR HONOR AT THE BOTTOM OF THE SEA."

A banquet! In his honor! The fox had never been to a banquet before. "How will I get there?" he asked.

"RIDE ON MY BACK," the whale said. He turned around so that the tip of his tail touched the sand. The fox ran up the whale's tail and leaped onto his back. Soon the whale was swimming toward the far horizon.

The fox enjoyed the voyage at first. Then the sea grew rough. Waves broke over the whale's back, soaking the fox to the skin. He looked back and saw the distant hills sinking below the horizon. He began having second thoughts.

"Will many guests be at the banquet?"

The whale chuckled. "NOT TOO MANY."

"I hope there is a lot to eat. Sea air always gives me an appetite."

The whale began to laugh. The fox did not like that at all. "What is so funny?" he asked.

"EVERYONE TALKS ABOUT HOW CLEVER YOU ARE, BUT I DON'T THINK YOU'RE CLEVER AT ALL. DID YOU REALLY THINK YOU WERE GOING TO A BANQUET?"

"Aren't I?"

"YES, BUT NOT AS A GUEST. YOU ARE TO BE THE MAIN COURSE!"

"You're joking!" the fox gasped.

"NOT AT ALL! KING LEVIATHAN INTENDS TO EAT YOUR HEART SO HE CAN BECOME AS CLEVER AS YOU ARE." The whale laughed so hard he made the sea bubble around him.

Poor fox. What could he do now? There appeared but little chance of

his escaping so far away from land. Still, he wasn't a fox for nothing.

"Oh dear, why didn't you tell me this at the beginning?" the fox said. "Had I known it was my heart Leviathan really wanted, I would have brought it with me."

The whale stopped in midocean. "ISN'T YOUR HEART INSIDE YOU?"

"Of course not! No fox ever carries his heart inside his body. The other animals would pursue us night and day if we did, for they all want to become as clever as we are. That is why every fox hides his heart in a secret place. I would have gladly given you mine had I known what you really wanted. Now I'm afraid it's too late. King Leviathan is going to be very angry."

The whale trembled at the thought of facing Leviathan's wrath. "WHAT WILL I DO? HOW WILL I EXPLAIN YOUR HEART IS NOT INSIDE YOUR BODY?"

The fox scratched his ears. "Wait! I have an idea. Turn around and swim back to shore as fast as you can. I will run and get my heart. Then you can take it to the king."

"THANK YOU, KIND FOX," the whale replied. He turned around and headed back toward land as fast as he could swim. The fox jumped from the whale's back as soon as the shore came in sight. He swam through the surf and ran up the beach.

"DON'T BE LONG. KING LEVIATHAN IS WAITING," the whale called to him.

He will wait a long time too, the fox thought to himself as he disappeared into the forest.

The fox never came back. He warned all the other foxes, and they in turn warned all their descendants not to go near the beach. To this day a fox is rarely seen at the seashore.

As for the whale, he waited and waited. When the fox failed to return, the whale wondered if he might have gotten lost. He began swimming up and down the beach, looking for him.

To this day that whale's descendants swim up and down the coast. People watching from the cliffs wonder why they travel so far, so tirelessly. The reason is they are still looking for the fox, hoping he will come back with his heart someday so they can all go home.

Fourth Night

SHAMMES

"*Show me something I have never seen before,*" *King Solomon said to Ashmodai, the king of the demons. Ashmodai reached down deep into the earth and pulled up a man with two heads.*

"*This is one of the descendants of Cain,*" *Ashmodai explained. "All Cainites, men and women, have two heads. They live in caverns deep underground.*"

Solomon spoke at length with the creature. Then he ordered Ashmodai to send him home.

"*I cannot,*" *Ashmodai said. "Once a Cainite leaves his cavern, he cannot return and live.*"

The two-headed man began to wail. "Woe!" the heads cried. "What will become of me?"

"*Do not weep,*" *said Solomon. "Since you were brought here at my command, I am responsible for you." Solomon took the Cainite into his service. In time the creature found a wife. Together they had seven sons. Six resembled their mother, having one head. The seventh took after his father, with two.*

In time the Cainite died, having amassed great wealth. His fortune was divided into seven portions, one for each of his sons.

The seventh son, the one with two heads, protested. "We are being robbed of our inheritance. There are two of us. Therefore we should have a double share."

"*Not so,*" *the other six sons replied. "You may have two heads, but you are still one person. You are entitled to only one share.*"

The seven sons came to Solomon seeking justice.

"Are you one person or two?" Solomon asked the seventh son.

"We are two," both heads replied.

"Come closer so I can examine you," Solomon said. The seventh son approached. Solomon suddenly slapped the right head across the cheek.

"Ow!" both heads cried.

"Two cry out, but only one is slapped," said Solomon. "One you are, and one you have always been. Take the single share your father left you and be content."

The Wonderful Shamir

King David was a man of war, but his son Solomon was a man of peace. For that reason the Lord granted Solomon the privilege of building the Holy Temple in Jerusalem.

The Lord gave Solomon the dimensions of the Temple. He described each gate, court, and chamber. He told Solomon how each was to be built and what materials were to be used in its construction. Finally the Lord said, "My Temple will be a House of Peace for humankind. No iron tool can be used to build it, for iron is a metal of war."

"How can my builders hew the great timbers for the ceiling? How can they split the stones for the walls without using iron tools?" Solomon asked.

But the Lord remained silent.

Solomon posed the problem to the wisest men in his kingdom. How

34

could the Temple be built without iron tools? No one knew.

Then Nathan the Prophet spoke. Nathan was a wise and holy man who had served Solomon's father David. "On the evening of the sixth day of Creation many marvels came into being. Among them was a wondrous creature called the shamir. The Lord fashioned it from beams of light. It is no bigger than a barleycorn, but it has the power to split massive stones. We could build the Temple easily with the help of the shamir."

"Where is the shamir to be found?" Solomon asked.

"No one knows," Nathan answered. "It is said that Ashmodai, king of the demons, has it. I do not know if that is true. No human being has entered the realm of the demons and returned alive."

Solomon pondered these words. "The Lord made the shamir for a purpose. If that purpose is to split stones for the Temple, then Ashmodai and all his demons cannot keep it from us."

Solomon summoned the captains of his army. "Which of you has the courage to seek out Ashmodai, king of the demons?"

Only Benayahu ben Yehoyada, the bravest man in Israel, stepped forward. "O Solomon, I am willing to seek out the king of the demons if you will use your wisdom to work out a plan."

"I have already done so," Solomon said.

Benayahu set out across the desert, for it is there that demons dwell. In addition to food and water, he carried a spade, a fleece, a jar of Greek wine, and an iron chain with a holy charm engraved on each link. He also carried Solomon's signet ring. The ring had the power to command the creatures of the earth as well as the spirits of the air.

Calling on the power of the ring, Benayahu summoned the spirits of the desert to guide him across the shifting sands. After many weeks he arrived at the foot of a black mountain. Halfway up the mountain Benayahu discovered a cistern covered with a heavy stone. At the top he found a cave strewn with human bones. Too weary to be frightened, Benayahu lay down among the bones and went to sleep.

He awoke to the sound of wings. They rattled overhead with a metallic buzz like the wings of locusts. Benayahu looked through the cave's entrance in time to see Ashmodai, king of the demons, land at the foot of the mountain.

The demon king possessed a terrifying beauty. He had two pairs of wings, transparent, like those of a dragonfly. Bronze feathers covered his body. They rattled like a coat of mail when he walked. His scaly legs ended in four toes, like the feet of a bird of prey. His face was birdlike too, with a powerful beak for tearing flesh, and fierce yellow eyes that burned like the desert sun.

Benayahu drew back into the cave as Ashmodai ascended the mountain. He paused at the cistern, pushed aside the stone, and drank. Then he spread his wings and flew off toward the east.

Benayahu worked quickly. Taking his spade, he dug a hole below the cistern so that the water ran out. He plugged the hole with the sheepskin and covered it with sand. Calling on Solomon's ring for strength, he moved the stone aside. After emptying the jar of Greek wine into the well, he pushed the stone back into place. Then he hid in the cave to await Ashmodai's return.

The demon appeared at sunset. He removed the stone and thrust his head into the well to drink.

"What is this?" Ashmodai exclaimed. He had never tasted wine before. "The water has a sweetish taste tonight. I like it." He lowered his head again and drank. Soon he was dancing around the well, laughing and singing. In a while his legs grew wobbly. His wings drooped, his eyelids closed. The king of the demons flopped down on the sand, fast asleep.

Benayahu dashed from the cave. He bound the demon with the magic chain and secured it with the power of Solomon's ring.

When Ashmodai awoke to find himself chained, he bellowed like the wild bull of Bashan. He struggled with demonic force, but the power of Solomon's ring held him fast. Benayahu approached cautiously. "Surrender yourself to Solomon, king of Israel," he told the demon.

"I bow to the power of Almighty God, Whose Name is written on this ring," Ashmodai snarled. "Were it not for that, no power on earth could hold me." He added slyly, "What does Solomon want of me?"

"He wishes to know where you have hidden a magical creature called the shamir."

Ashmodai laughed. "That secret is for Solomon's ears alone."

"Then you must accompany me to Jerusalem," Benayahu said.

The journey took several weeks. All the inhabitants of Jerusalem turned out to cheer Benayahu and to see the dreaded Ashmodai being led before King Solomon. The king of Israel addressed the king of the demons:

"The Lord wishes me to build a Temple in Jerusalem. No iron tool may be used in its building, since iron is a metal of war, and God's house must be a house of peace. I have recently learned of a fabulous creature called the shamir. I am told it has the power to split the hardest stone. This creature was entrusted to your care, Ashmodai. The time has come to give it up. We need the shamir to split the great stones for the Temple. By the power of my ring, I command you to surrender the shamir."

Ashmodai replied with scorn, "Your power is useless. You cannot force me to give up something I do not possess. The shamir is no longer in my keeping. I used it for mischief: for splitting mountains, for making rivers run backward. The Lord realized His mistake in entrusting the shamir to me. He took it away. Where it is now, I know not."

"Alas! Was my effort in vain?" Benayahu asked.

"Not at all," said Solomon. "The end of the quest is at hand. We know where the shamir is not. Now we must find where it is."

Such power as the shamir possessed could not remain hidden forever. Signs of its presence must exist somewhere.

Calling upon the power of his ring, Solomon summoned a council of the birds, for they among all living things travel farthest and see most. All the feathered creatures of the earth, from the great eagle to the tiny hummingbird, came before Solomon's throne. Speaking in the language of the birds, Solomon told them about the shamir and explained why he needed it to build the Temple. He asked if any of them, in their flights over land or sea, had seen signs of such a creature.

The birds shook their heads. None of them had seen anything like the shamir.

A giant albatross stepped forward. Spreading her matchless wings, the bird bowed to the king. "O Solomon," she said, "we albatrosses are creatures of sea and air. We come on land only to lay our eggs. No other bird flies as far or as wide as we do. I have never heard of this 'shamir.' Yet I remember once a sudden storm blew me far to the north, to the icy seas at the top of the world. There I met a strange bird that nests on a rock in the middle of the ocean. This 'storm bird'—for so it calls itself—builds its nest in a crack in the rock. As its chicks grow larger, it widens the crack by chipping away the rock with a peculiar object no bigger than a barleycorn. Could this be the shamir?"

It certainly could! And what safer place for it than on a rock in the middle of the ocean? But how to recover it?

Solomon asked the albatross, "Can you carry my servant Benayahu to that rock in the northern sea?"

"If he has the courage to ride on my back, I can."

"Then I have a plan," Solomon said.

Solomon gave Benayahu a piece of clear glass wrapped in silk to protect it on the journey. Clutching the package, Benayahu climbed upon the albatross's back. The great bird spread her wings. She circled twice, then veered off toward the north.

Benayahu and the albatross flew north for forty days. Buffeted by stormy winds, drenched by icy seas, the hero and the gallant bird finally reached the lonely rock. Benayahu climbed down from the summit. He found the storm bird's nest sheltered in a crack. Three tiny chicks stretched their mouths wide, demanding food. Benayahu unwrapped the piece of glass and placed it on top of the nest. Then he mounted the albatross and flew high into the air. There they circled, waiting for the mother bird's return.

In a little while the storm bird arrived with food for her chicks. She heard them peeping; she saw them stretching their necks toward her, but when she tried to feed them she found something in the way. It was the glass. The storm bird pecked at the invisible barrier. Then she flew off. She returned, carrying a shining object no bigger than a barleycorn. She placed it on the glass. The glass split in two.

The albatross swooped down from the sky. Benayahu snatched the object from the storm bird. He and the albatross flew swiftly south, leaving the lonely rock far behind.

Benayahu and the albatross returned to Jerusalem. King Solomon praised the hero and the bird. He examined the mysterious object they brought. Was it really the shamir?

Solomon placed the object on a block of marble. The heavy stone split in two. The shamir had been found.

And so Solomon built the Temple as God commanded, without iron tools of any kind. When the building was complete, Solomon gave the shamir to the albatross. He told her to return it to the storm bird's keeping.

There it has remained, on that lonely rock in the middle of the northern sea. There it will remain until the Messiah comes and a new Temple arises in Jerusalem.

SHAMMES

*T*he people of Chelm have a logic all their own. Once two Chelmers went for a walk. It started to rain.

"Open your umbrella so we won't get wet," one said to the other.

"It won't do any good," his companion replied. "My old umbrella is full of holes. It leaks like a sieve."

"Then why did you bring it?"

"I didn't think it would rain."

Did the Rabbi Have a Head?

The rabbi of Chelm was a wise and holy man who spent nearly every waking hour in his study, pondering the sacred texts, meditating on God's word. As a result, though the people of Chelm loved and respected him, few had ever seen his face.

Every morning the rabbi would get up before dawn and walk to the river to bathe. Then he would dry himself, dress, and return to town, arriving at the synagogue in time for morning prayers.

One morning he failed to appear. The people of Chelm searched everywhere, but they could discover no clue as to where the rabbi might have gone or what might have befallen him. All they found were his clothes, folded neatly under a tree.

A month passed. No trace of the rabbi turned up. Then a fisherman made a horrifying discovery. He found a corpse entangled in his net. The corpse's head was missing.

The people of Chelm came rushing to the river. Could this be the body of their beloved rabbi?

The town coroner examined the remains. In his report he wrote, "This corpse resembles our dear rabbi in some ways, but not in others. Most important, my examination reveals that the person to whom this body belonged did not have a head. If our rabbi had a head, then this cannot be his body. On the other hand, if he did not have a head, then it could be."

All of Chelm struggled with this question. Did the rabbi have a head? Since they so seldom saw him, no one remembered if he did or not. They asked the people who knew him best.

"Did the rabbi have a head?" they asked the cantor at the synagogue. "To tell the truth, I'm not sure," the cantor replied. "Whenever the rabbi prayed, he covered himself up with his prayer shawl, so I don't know whether he had a head or not. If he did, I never saw it. But he did have feet. I saw them many times. He had two."

The bathhouse attendant said, "I know what all the men in town look like with their clothes on or off. Except the rabbi. He was an extremely modest man. He came and went so quietly that most of the time I hardly knew he was here. When he went in the steam bath, he always sat on the highest bench, where the steam is so thick you can't see anything. So whether he had a head or not, I can't say. But he did have a *tukhis*.* I saw that plenty of times."

They asked the rabbi's wife. "Did your husband have a head? Think! It's important. Try to remember."

The poor woman's eyes were still red from weeping. "Friends, what can I say? I don't know if my husband had a head or not. He studied all the

---

*Backside.

time. I never saw him. Wait! I do remember something. I can't say for sure if he had a head, but I am positive that he had a nose. He used to take snuff. When I passed his door, I often heard him sneeze."

Did the rabbi of Chelm have a head? The evidence was inconclusive. Not knowing what else to do, the people of Chelm gathered up everything connected with the case and sent it to the Grand Rabbi of Vilna. The Grand Rabbi of Vilna was the wisest man in the world. If anyone were able to decide whether or not the rabbi of Chelm had a head, it would certainly be he.

Six months later the Grand Rabbi replied:

"After examining the evidence in this case, I have come to the following conclusion:

"The rabbi of Chelm definitely had a head. On the other hand, whether any of the citizens of Chelm do remains open for discussion."

SHAMMES

A long time ago there lived in the city of Dubno a famous rabbi who was known for his eloquence. Wherever he went, crowds of people gathered to hear his sermons. They called him the "Dubner Maggid" or "The Preacher of Dubno."

The maggid seldom stayed in one place for long. He traveled from town to town in a fine coach drawn by prancing horses. His coachman was a peasant named Ivan. Ivan was a jolly fellow. He couldn't read or write, but he was a fine coachman all the same. He was ready to drive day or night, over the worst roads, in all kinds of weather. He kept the coach and harness in good repair and made sure that the horses were always in top condition. Ivan and the maggid had traveled together for years. The maggid thought of Ivan as one of his best friends.

One day, as the coach rolled along the road, the maggid noticed that Ivan was strangely silent.

"Ivan, is something wrong?" the maggid asked. "You're always telling jokes or singing songs. Why are you so quiet?"

Ivan answered, "Well, Maggid, if you must know, there is something on my mind. But it's only foolishness. I shouldn't trouble you with it."

The maggid replied, "Ivan, you've been my coachman for thirty years. If something is disturbing you, I want to know about it. I might not be able to help, but at least I can listen."

"All right, here it is," said Ivan. "But as I told you, it's only foolishness. Whenever we come to a town, Maggid, all the people come out to greet you. They listen to every word you speak. They seat you in the place of honor. It's

47

like that everywhere we go. As for me, I'm only the coachman. Nobody pays attention to me. They look at me as if I weren't there. Once—just once—I would like people to notice me. I want to know what it feels like to be treated with respect. If I could experience that, I would never ask for another thing."

"Well, Ivan, what you're asking for is no simple matter. You are you and I am I. How could it ever be different?" the maggid said.

"I know a way," said Ivan. "We'll be arriving in Tarnopol in another hour. You've never been there before. Nobody in Tarnopol knows what the Dubner Maggid looks like. If we were to exchange clothes, if I were to ride in the coach while you rode up front holding the reins, nobody in Tarnopol would be able to tell who was really the coachman and who was the maggid."

"That's clever, Ivan," the maggid said. "There's just one problem. Have you thought about what you will do if the people of Tarnopol ask you a question?"

"What do you mean?" Ivan asked.

"What I mean is: just wearing a rabbi's coat doesn't make you a rabbi. You have to study the holy books from the time you are a child. You have to know them by heart; you have to know how to interpret them correctly. You've never been to school, Ivan. You can't read or write. If the people of Tarnopol ask you a question, how will you answer? Have you given that any thought?"

"Don't worry, Maggid," Ivan said. "I'll think of something."

Ivan stopped the coach. He and the maggid exchanged clothes. Then, with Ivan inside dressed as the maggid and the maggid up in the driver's box dressed as a coachman, the coach continued on to Tarnopol.

The people of Tarnopol swarmed out to greet the Dubner Maggid. Of course, they paid no attention to the real maggid, who was seated in the driver's box. Instead, with great rejoicing, they escorted Ivan the coach-man to the synagogue where a sumptuous banquet awaited. They seated Ivan on the dais, in the seat of honor. The coachman's face beamed with pleasure. His greatest wish had come true.

After the meal was over and the dishes had been cleared away, the rabbis of Tarnopol gathered around their honored guest. "Maggid," they said, "a difficult question arose a month ago when we were studying together. Since then we have tried to explain it, but without success. Perhaps with your great learning you can enlighten us with the answer."

The real maggid had to keep himself from laughing as he watched unnoticed from the doorway. It was just as he predicted. Poor Ivan! What will he do now? *the maggid thought.*

"What is your question?" Ivan asked. The rabbis told him.

"Is that all?" Ivan rose from his chair and began shouting angrily. "Do you think I came all the way from Dubno to waste my time with such easy questions? How dare you call yourselves rabbis if you can't even answer that? Look, here is my coachman Ivan standing in the doorway. He hasn't been to school one day in his life; he can't read or write. He isn't even Jewish! But Ivan can answer that question. Ivan, come up here and answer this easy question for these so-called rabbis!"

So, of course, to the astonishment of the people of Tarnopol, "Ivan" did.

Thereafter, wherever the maggid traveled, not only was he honored as a great scholar, but so was his coachman Ivan!

The Caliph and
the Cobbler

Over a thousand years ago a great caliph ruled in the city of Baghdad. The emperors of Rome and Cathay, with all their wealth, could not rival the splendor of his court.

The caliph had an unusual habit. Every evening he took off his silk robes and dressed himself in the rough clothing of a wandering dervish. Thus disguised, he roamed the streets of Baghdad from twilight to dawn, mingling with the common people.

It so happened that one night the caliph wandered into the Dahar Al-Yahud, the Jewish quarter of Baghdad. The houses were dark, for most of the people had gone to bed. The caliph noticed a lamp burning in the

50

window of a shabby hut. He knocked on the door. A man opened it.

"Peace be upon you," the caliph said. "I am a stranger in this city. Would you mind having a guest for the evening?"

"A guest is a gift from God!" the man exclaimed, inviting him in. The two men shared a meager meal of bread and lentils.

"You must tell me your name so I can thank you properly," the caliph said.

"My name is Aaron," the man answered.

"Do you have a trade, Aaron?"

"I am a cobbler, after a fashion."

"How so?"

"I repair shoes and sandals. From this I earn enough each day to buy a dinner of bread and lentils."

"What would you do if you could no longer practice your trade?"

"I praise the Lord, day by day. He has always looked after me. I expect He will continue to do so," Aaron said.

"We will see," the caliph murmured to himself.

The next morning the caliph issued a decree forbidding cobblers to repair shoes or sandals. That night, after putting on his disguise, he went directly to the house of Aaron the cobbler.

Aaron greeted him at the door. "Come in, my friend. A guest is a gift from God."

"I was worried about you," the caliph said. "Have you heard of the new decree forbidding cobblers to repair shoes or sandals?"

"Oh yes. But that didn't trouble me. I managed to get by."

"What did you do?"

"I borrowed a bucket from my neighbor and went to the well. I worked as a water carrier, bringing water to people's houses. I worked hard, but I earned enough to buy my dinner."

"I see," the caliph said. "But what if you were unable to practice this trade?"

"I praise the Lord, day by day," Aaron said.

Indeed, the caliph thought.

The next day the caliph issued another decree outlawing the trade of water carrier. The people of Baghdad now had to draw and carry water for themselves.

That evening the caliph made his way once more to the home of Aaron the cobbler. Aaron greeted him at the door.

"Come in, my friend. A guest is a gift from God."

The caliph handed him a package of dates. "I was worried that you might not eat tonight. Have you heard the new decree? The trade of water carrier is now forbidden."

"I know," Aaron replied. "But never fear. I found another way to earn my bread."

"What did you do?"

"I worked as a woodcutter. I borrowed an ax from my neighbor. I walked to the forest beyond the city. There I cut a load of firewood. I carried it back to town and sold it for enough money to buy my dinner."

"Cleverly done. But what would happen if you could no longer practice that trade?" the caliph asked.

Aaron looked him steadily in the eye. "Praise the Lord, day by day."

The caliph nodded. "Amen."

The next day the caliph issued another decree. All the woodcutters in Baghdad had to report to the palace to be sworn in as members of the royal guard.

That evening, the caliph came again to the house of Aaron the cobbler.

"Come in, my friend. A guest is a gift from God."

"How did you get by today?" the caliph asked. "I heard that all the woodcutters in the city were drafted into the royal guard."

"Indeed we were," Aaron replied. "I had to report to the palace this morning. The captain of the guard gave me a sword and stationed me before the caliph's gate. I had to stand there all day. Of course, I couldn't earn any money doing that. However, as I was going home, I passed a swordsmith's shop. The smith offered to buy my blade, so I sold it to him. No one will know. I kept the hilt. The smith replaced the sword's steel blade with a wooden one."

The caliph shook his head. "Aaron, aren't you taking a terrible chance? What will happen if the caliph calls upon you to use your sword?"

"Praise the Lord, day by day. That will never happen," Aaron said.

The caliph replied, "I hope not."

The next morning the caliph summoned his chief minister, the grand vizier.

"Wretch!" the caliph screamed, striking him across the face. "I know you are plotting against me. You will pay for your treachery with your life!"

"Mercy!" the terrified vizier cried.

"Summon the guard from the gate!"

The guard came running. It was Aaron the cobbler.

"Guard," the caliph said, pointing to the vizier, "draw your sword. Cut off this traitor's head."

"There must be some mistake! I am innocent!" the vizier wailed.

Aaron turned as pale as the vizier. Trembling, he bowed to the caliph. "O Caliph, I have never killed a man before. I don't know what to do. May I say a prayer first?"

"As you wish, but don't be long about it."

Aaron raised his eyes toward heaven. "Lord, I am only a humble cobbler. I have never harmed another human being in my life. The caliph has ordered me to cut off the vizier's head, yet the vizier swears he is innocent. Lord, let my hands not be stained with innocent blood. If the

vizier is guilty, may my sword be sharpened steel. But if he is innocent, turn my blade to wood!"

Aaron drew his sword. Lo and behold, the blade was wood. "Praise the Lord!" Aaron exclaimed.

"Day by day," the caliph added, revealing himself as Aaron's midnight guest.

Aaron the cobbler received a rich reward. The caliph revoked his decrees, so that cobblers, water carriers, and woodcutters could earn their livings. This, however, no longer affected Aaron, for with the caliph's friendship and the vizier's gratitude, he never again had to labor for his dinner.

Thus it is truly said that the Lord helps those who praise Him.

Day by day.

Seventh Night

SHAMMES

*D*id you hear about the robbery? The news was all over Kiev. A thief broke into the Imperial Bank in the middle of the night and made off with all the money. The police didn't have a clue. A big reward—a hundred rubles—was offered to anyone who could solve the crime.

Hershel's ears pricked up at the word "reward." He headed for the police station.

"I can find out who robbed the bank," he told the policemen.

"Who are you?" the chief of police asked.

"I am the famous detective, Hershel of Ostropol. If anyone can find the culprit, I can. But first I must examine the scene of the crime."

"Take him down to the bank. Give him all the help he needs," the police chief told his men.

The policemen drove Hershel down to the bank. Hershel examined the doors, the windows, the locks, the plundered vault. Then he told the policemen: "This was a professional job. I want you to round up all the known burglars and safecrackers in Kiev and bring them here so I can have a look at them."

By late afternoon the policemen had all the professional criminals in Kiev assembled in the lobby. Hershel went down the line, inspecting each one. Then he announced,

"I know who the culprit is. The rest of you can go."

The criminals started for the door.

"Stop!" Hershel cried. "Who said anything about you?"

One man stopped in his tracks.

"Aha," Hershel told the policemen, "there's your robber!"

They questioned him, and sure enough, he confessed.

Detective Hershel got his reward.

When Hershel Eats

Years ago a wealthy miser lived in the city of Lemberg. His name was Reb Shimon Kamtzan. It was bad enough that he never gave anything to charity, but what made him especially despicable was how he took pleasure in tormenting the poor.

One of his favorite tricks was to invite a poor person to his house for Friday night dinner. Reb Shimon would seat his guest at the far end of a long table. All the food was placed at Reb Shimon's end, forcing the poor guest to reach down the table in order to get anything to eat. Even if his guest did succeed in taking a small portion, Reb Shimon would keep pestering him with questions that the guest would have to answer in order to appear polite. After a few minutes the servants would come and clear the table before the poor visitor had a chance to eat anything. At that point Reb Shimon would shake his head and sigh, "Too bad you weren't hungry. It was a delicious dinner."

Once it happened that Hershel of Ostropol arrived in Lemberg one Friday afternoon. As luck would have it, Reb Shimon noticed him at the synagogue and, thinking to amuse himself at the expense of another ragged beggar, invited him home for dinner. Hershel naturally accepted. "Don't go, he only wants to torture you," the other beggars said. They warned Hershel about Reb Shimon's tricks.

"All the more reason to go," Hershel said. "This *paskudniak** needs to be taught a lesson."

Everything at Reb Shimon's house happened just the way the beggars predicted. There was a long table in the dining room with two chairs at either end. Hershel sat down in one, Reb Shimon in the other. The servants brought the meal to the table: chicken soup, gefilte fish, roast chicken, noodle pudding, white challah hot from the oven, and a bottle of expensive wine. They placed all the food before Reb Shimon. That didn't discourage Hershel. He got up from his chair, piled his plate high with food, took the platters back to his end of the table, and began to eat. Reb Shimon stood up and sputtered with annoyance, but what could he say? He tried his second trick.

"I hear, Reb Hershel, that you come from Ostropol. I have a cousin who lives in Ostropol. Maybe you know him? Reb Moishe Pipik?"

Hershel cleaned his plate and filled it again. "He's dead."

The news shocked Reb Shimon. "Dead? I can't believe it. Why didn't his wife let me know?"

"She's dead too."

"What? How can she be dead? She was a young woman. What happened to their three children? Who's taking care of them?"

"Nobody. They're dead."

"All dead? Those beautiful children! Oh my! What a tragedy!"

---

*Scoundrel.

Hershel finished the noodle pudding and started on the chicken.

"What happened to his business?" Reb Shimon asked. "I lent my cousin a lot of money. Is his partner going to pay me back?"

"Who knows? He's dead too."

Reb Shimon turned pale. "Also dead? What about my cousin's brother-in-law Mendel? Mendel would know something."

Hershel swallowed the last of the gefilte fish. "Mendel's dead."

"Mendel too? Heaven help us! As soon as the Sabbath is over, I'll write to the rabbi in Ostropol. The rabbi always knows what's going on. He'll be able to help me."

"No, he won't," said Hershel. "He's dead."

"Dead!" Reb Shimon cried. "Is everyone in Ostropol dead? What terrible catastrophe happened there?"

"Nothing happened there," said Hershel as he poured the last of the wine. "It's just that when Hershel of Ostropol eats, the whole world may as well be dead. Too bad you weren't hungry, Reb Shimon. It was a delicious dinner."

Eighth Night

SHAMMES

*R*abbi Elimelech of Lizhansk and his brother, Rabbi Zusya of Hanipol, spent most of their lives walking from town to town, bringing their followers words of comfort and wisdom. As the years went by and the two brothers grew older, traveling over rough roads in all kinds of weather became difficult for them. One of their followers, a wealthy man, offered to hire a coach and a team of horses to take Elimelech and Zusya wherever they wanted to go. At first the two brothers would have nothing to do with the idea, for they were simple men who refused to indulge themselves with luxuries. Their followers, however, pleaded with them to accept the gift, so eventually they did.

Now living in the town of Brody was a certain merchant named Reb Arele. He had no use for Rabbi Elimelech, Rabbi Zusya, or their followers. He laughed at their ragged clothes. "Tramps! Parasites!" he called them. In all the years Elimelech and Zusya had been coming to Brody, he had not offered them so much as one friendly word.

But this year, when Reb Arele saw the two brothers riding into town in a fine coach drawn by a high-stepping team, he was greatly impressed. He had his secretary write a polite letter to Elimelech and Zusya, inviting them to stay at his house as his guests while they were in town. Rabbi Elimelech read the letter. Then he sat down and wrote this reply:

My dear Reb Arele:

Thank you for your kind letter. However, my brother and I are unsure what to make of it. In all the years we have been coming to

61

Brody, you never once greeted us with even a simple "Shalom." Now you are inviting us to stay in your home as your guests.

What could have made the difference?

My brother and I are the same as we were before. We haven't become wiser or worthier. The only difference we can see is that this time we arrived in a coach, whereas before we came on foot. Therefore, it must be the coach and the horses that impress you.

Since that is the case, we will leave the coach at your house. I know you will be happy to entertain the horses as your special guests. But as for Zusya and myself, we will stay with our old friends as we have always done."

The Spotted Pony

There was a wedding in Kolomea. Bronya, the daughter of Reb Yudel, the timber merchant, married the son of the rabbi of Belz. What a wedding it was! No one could recall its like in the history of the town. Reb Itzik, the wagon driver, spent the week bringing in guests from the surrounding villages. A klezmer band played throughout the night. What music! What musicians! A fiddler played with them, a tiny man in a worn coat so full of patches it seemed all speckled and spotted. His fiddle sang as if it were alive. "He has magic in his fingers, that one," everyone agreed.

The party lasted three days. When it ended, Reb Itzik drove the musicians on to the next town. Along the way the fiddler suddenly became ill. Reb Itzik and the other musicians laid him down in the back of the wagon. The fiddler's clothes were soaked with sweat, as if he had been pulled from the river, but his skin felt burning hot, like the top of a stove.

"We must call a doctor. This man is too sick to go on," Reb Itzik told the musicians.

"What can we do?" they cried. "We are poor musicians. We have no money for doctors. We hardly know where we will sleep tonight ourselves."

"The fiddler can stay with me until he recovers," Reb Itzik said. So while the other musicians continued on foot, Reb Itzik turned his wagon around and brought the fiddler back to Kolomea. He sent for the doctor as soon as he arrived. The doctor listened to the fiddler's heart and took his pulse. Then he told Reb Itzik, "This man is beyond help."

"Can nothing be done?"

"Make him comfortable. Do whatever you can to ease his last moments."

After the doctor left, the fiddler said to Reb Itzik, "I know I am dying. My soul is heavy because I cannot repay your kindness. You have taken me into your house, nursed me in your own bed, called a doctor at your expense. In a few days you will have to bury me, and I have no way of repaying you."

"You do not have to repay me," Reb Itzik told him. "Good deeds are their own reward. I will pray for your recovery. God will work a miracle."

The fiddler shook his head. "There will be no miracles. But you can ease my soul by doing what I ask. Write an account of what my illness has cost you. Make it out to the last penny. When I am dead, take my fiddle and sell it. It will bring enough money to repay you. Do this for me. Promise you will sell the fiddle."

Reb Itzik promised. He wrote out an account for all his expenses. The fiddler folded the paper and wove it between the fiddle's strings. Three days later he died. The whole town came to his funeral. He didn't lie in a pauper's grave. Reb Itzik saw to that. But he never sold the fiddle. He set it on a high shelf and forgot about it.

One year passed. One bright day, as Reb Itzik drove along the river, he came upon a speckled pony standing in the road. The pony wore neither saddle nor bridle. There was no way to identify his owner.

"Don't worry, little pony, I'll find out where you belong." Reb Itzik tied the pony to the back of his wagon and drove on to the next village. He asked if anyone recognized the pony. No one had ever seen the animal before. It was the same in the next town, and the next. When Reb Itzik reached home, he put the mysterious pony in a stall.

"I can care for him till his owner turns up," Reb Itzik decided. But weeks passed and no owner appeared. The speckled pony remained in his stall.

Summer turned to autumn. Early one morning Reb Itzik went out to harness his horses. He found Lozhik, his best horse, lame. His second horse, Ferdka, looked ill. What now? Sick and lame horses cannot pull a wagon. Just then, the speckled pony whinnied, as if to say, "What about me?"

Why not? thought Reb Itzik. *A pony can pull a light load. That's better than none at all.* He hitched the speckled pony to the wagon and started off. Soon he exclaimed in surprise, "Why, this pony is as strong as Lozhik! And quick, like Ferdka. He does the work of two horses!" Reb Itzik never had to touch the reins. The speckled pony knew exactly where to go.

From then on he worked the three horses in turn. He still cherished Lozhik and Ferdka, but the speckled pony became his favorite.

Now Reb Itzik was a disciple of that great and holy man, Rabbi Israel of the Good Name. Rabbi Israel traveled around the countryside visiting his followers, helping with their troubles. Sometimes he worked miracles.

Rabbi Israel arrived in Kolomea on Hanukkah eve. He stopped at Reb Itzik's house. Knowing how much Rabbi Israel loved horses, Reb Itzik told him about the spotted pony.

"Show me this animal," Rabbi Israel said. Together they went out to the stable. Lozhik and Ferdka lowered their heads so the rabbi could scratch their ears, but the spotted pony positively pranced for joy. Rabbi Israel turned to Reb Itzik and said, "Give me this pony as a Hanukkah gift."

Reb Itzik replied, "The pony is not mine to give. Even if he were, I could not do it. I would miss him too much."

Rabbi Israel shrugged. "It is no great matter."

When they returned to the house, Rabbi Israel noticed a fiddle resting on a shelf above the clothes chest.

"Since when do you play the fiddle?"

"I don't," Reb Itzik replied.

"Then why is this fiddle in your house?"

Reb Itzik told him the sad story of the fiddler. "I did what I could for that poor soul."

"But you never sold the fiddle," Rabbi Israel said.

"No," Reb Itzik admitted, "I never got around to doing it."

Rabbi Israel took the fiddle down from the shelf. A piece of paper fell out. A long column of numbers was written on it. "What is this?" Rabbi Israel asked.

Reb Itzik shrugged. "The fiddler insisted on writing out his debt as a loan to be repaid. I did not take it seriously. He slipped the paper into the fiddle before he died. I forgot it was there."

Rabbi Israel turned to Reb Itzik. "Tonight is the first night of Hanukkah. Give me this paper as a gift."

"Rabbi, it is a worthless piece of paper! The man is long dead."

"Do as I say. Drop the paper into my hands and repeat after me: 'I, Reb Itzik, of my own free will, hereby transfer this debt to Rabbi Israel of the Good Name.' "

Reb Itzik repeated the words. Rabbi Israel held up the paper.

"And I, Rabbi Israel of the Good Name, hereby declare the fiddler's debt paid in full." He tore the paper into seven pieces and threw them in

the stove. They vanished in the flames. He turned to Reb Itzik. "Show me your horses."

A bewildered Reb Itzik led the way back to the stable. Lozhik and Ferdka stamped their hooves. The spotted pony's stall stood empty.

"My pony is gone!" Reb Itzik cried.

"Your pony has returned home," Rabbi Israel said. "Miracles fill this night. Reb Itzik, know that your pony was none but the poor fiddler, returned from the grave. Unable to rest, he took a pony's form so he could work for you."

"Why should he do that? I asked nothing of him."

"He demanded it of himself. Throughout his life this fiddler always paid his debts. What pained him most as he lay dying was knowing he could not repay you. So he gave you his fiddle. Once you sold it, he could rest in peace. But you did not sell it. The debt remained unpaid. And so the fiddler returned as the spotted pony to work for you until he paid his debt. He worked willingly, because the harder he worked, the sooner he would be free. He might have gone on working for years."

"How did you know?" Reb Itzik asked.

"I could see it in his face," Rabbi Israel answered. "I could not leave that soul in distress. I had to set him free. Since you would not give me the pony, I canceled the debt. Do not grieve for him. His soul is where it belongs. He is at peace."

Reb Itzik shuddered, but not from the cold. Rabbi Israel wiped the mud from his boots. "Let us go back inside. It is time to light the Hanukkah candles."

"In a moment, Rabbi. I would like to sit here awhile."

"As you wish."

Reb Itzik sat alone in the darkness, thinking about the fiddler and the spotted pony. Finally he rose, shut the empty stall, and started back to the house. He saw the menorah standing in the window, waiting to be lit.

Bright stars twinkled in the sky overhead, each one a candle in the menorah of heaven. Reb Itzik stopped. He heard music. The bright strains of a klezmer's fiddle lifted his heart. Each note hung in the night air like a shining star.

Reb Itzik paused on the doorstep, drinking in the joyous melody. He entered the house as the last note faded. "Rabbi Israel, you play so well! Take the fiddle as a Hanukkah gift."

Rabbi Israel's eyes turned to the klezmer's fiddle resting in its old place above the clothes chest.

"Reb Itzik, surely you know me better than that. What would I do with a fiddle? I cannot play a note."

Heaven and Hell

What is heaven like?

In heaven the righteous sit at a great banquet. The table is set with every imaginable delicacy. People in heaven have but to stretch out their arms to take whatever they desire.

However, in heaven people's arms do not bend at the elbow.

What is hell like?

In hell the wicked sit at a great banquet. The table is set with every imaginable delicacy. People in hell have but to stretch out their arms to take whatever they desire.

However, in hell people's arms also do not bend at the elbow.

So what is the difference between heaven and hell?

People in heaven feed each other.